HOW TO DRAW
FALL THINGS

for kids

ALLI KOCH

Paige Tate & co.

Copyright © 2025 by Alli Koch
Published by Paige Tate & Co.
Paige Tate & Co. is an imprint of Blue Star Press
PO Box 8835, Bend, OR 97708
contact@paigetate.com
www.paigetate.com

All rights reserved. No part of this publication may be reproduced or transmitted in any form or by any means, electronic or mechanical, including photocopy, recording, or any information storage and retrieval system, without permission in writing from the publisher.

Written and illustrated by Alli Koch

Printed in Colombia

10 9 8 7 6 5 4 3 2 1

The authorized representative in the EU for product safety and compliance is Authorised Rep Compliance Ltd., Ground Floor, 71 Lower Baggot Street, Dublin, D02 P593, Ireland.
www.arccompliance.com

ISBN: 9781963183108

INTRO	5
TOOLS	6
BREAK IT DOWN	7
FALL THINGS	9
NATURE IN FALL	29
THE HOLIDAYS	45
CREATE YOUR OWN	73

LET'S DRAW!

The nice thing about being an artist is that you can make the rules. Everyone has their own style, which is why your drawings will look different from someone else's. In this book, each project is broken down into easy-to-follow steps. My goal is to help you see the simple parts of what may seem like a hard thing to draw.

We will start with the most basic outline or guide and work our way up. You will start to see a pattern with each fall thing we draw, starting with simple guidelines, then breaking down "C" and "S" shaped lines, and lastly erasing the unneeded lines for the finished look. Don't forget to draw your lines lightly first so it is easier to erase them. My favorite thing to say when drawing is:

If it was perfect, it would not look handmade!

I cannot wait for you to get started. Happy drawing!

TOOLS

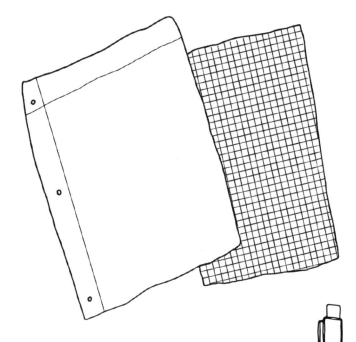

The cool thing about art is that you can use any tool you want! Yep, that's right! You are the artist, so feel free to be creative. For this book, let's keep it simple. It's easy to learn using either blank sheets of paper or grid paper.

When you are learning to draw, you really only need a pencil and a good eraser. To follow the step-by-step instructions, draw everything lightly, then go over your lines with whatever tool you would like to use. You could use different pens, markers, colored pencils, or even crayons to add details to your drawings.

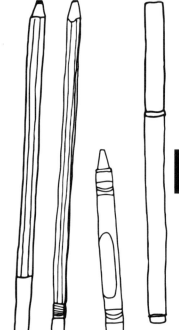

CIRCLES CAN BE TRICKY. TRY USING A PENNY OR A CIRCLE STENCIL TO HELP!

BREAK IT DOWN

Anyone can draw! If you can write your ABCs (which I am pretty sure you can do!), then you can draw everything in this book. Each project can be broken down into a bunch of "C" and "S" shaped lines. Almost anything that is round is two simple "C" shaped lines put together. An "S" shaped line is for when something has a dip or curvy line.

Most of the projects in this book are broken down into six or eight steps. What you need to draw in each step will appear as a black line; what you have already drawn will appear as gray lines. There are more than 40 fall-themed illustrations in this book for you to learn how to draw. The chapter dividers in this book are also bonus coloring pages that you can color!

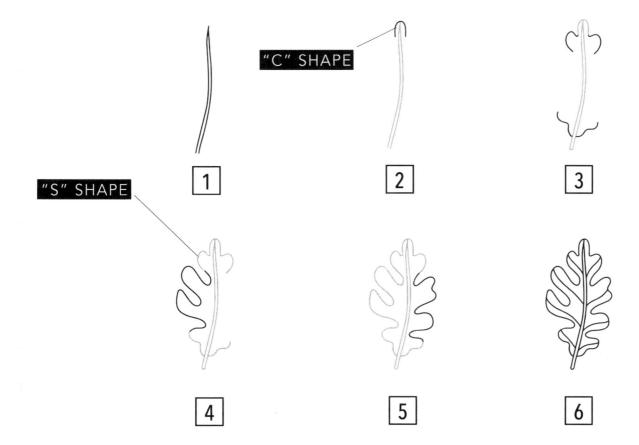

FALL THINGS

SCHOOL BUS

Before the first motor-powered school bus was introduced in 1914, children would either walk to school or take a horse-drawn carriage ride.

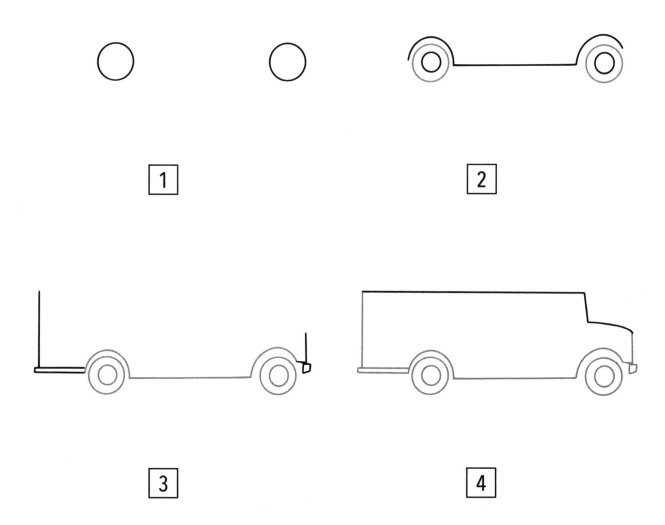

SCHOOLHOUSE

The oldest-standing schoolhouse in the US was built in the early 1700s in St. Augustine, Florida.

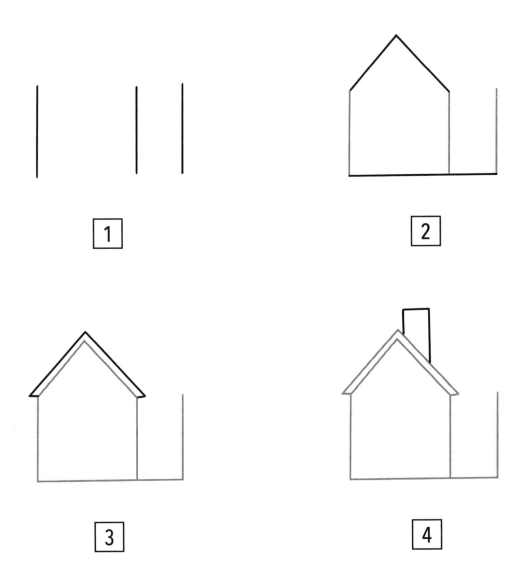

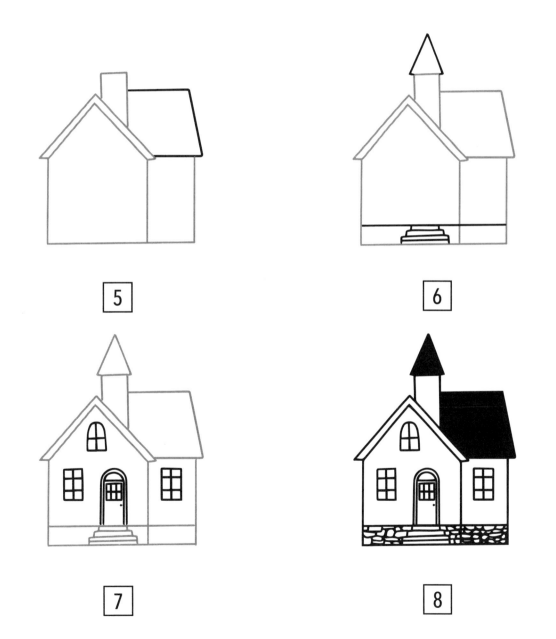

PLAYGROUND

The first playground in the US opened in 1887 in San Francisco's Golden Gate Park.

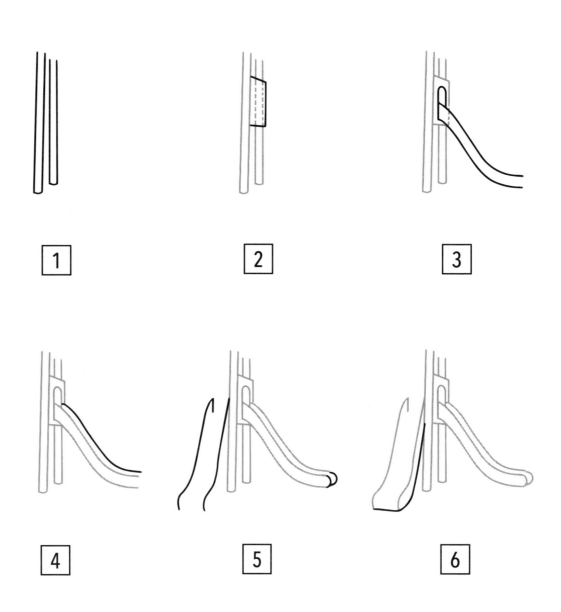

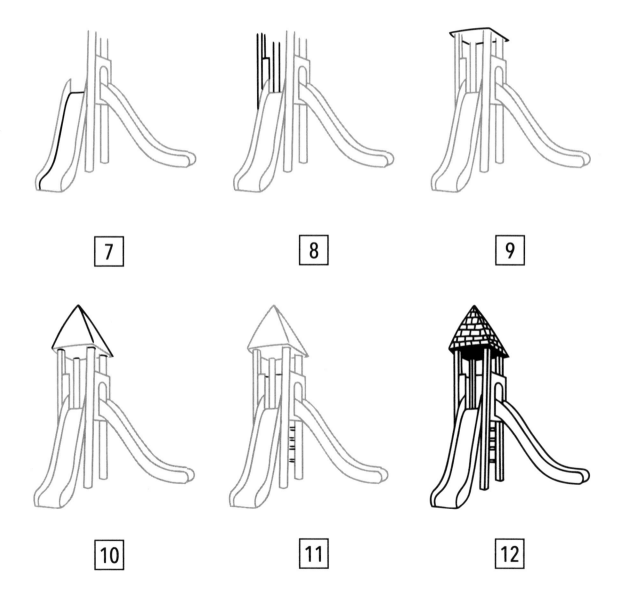

BACKPACK

Around the world, there are many different names for a backpack, including *knapsack*, *rucksack*, *pack*, and *haversack*.

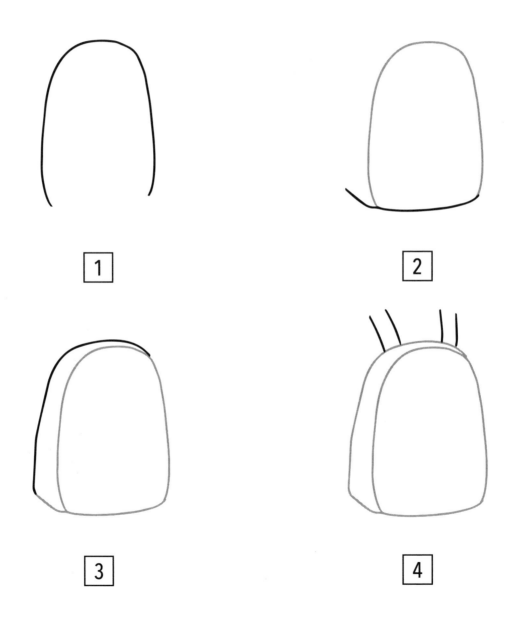

CANDY APPLE

According to bakers, crisp and tart apple varieties, like Fuji and Granny Smith, make for the best candy apples.

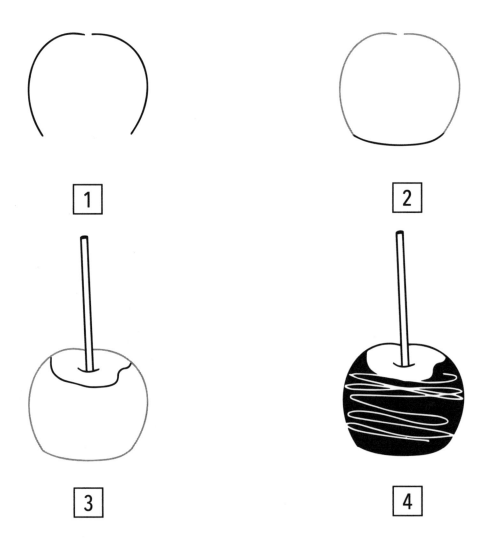

SCARECROW

In Nagoro, a small village in Japan, there are more scarecrows than residents!

FOOTBALL

Although it's known as *football*, players mainly use their hands to throw the ball! Only one position—the kicker—primarily uses their feet to transport the ball.

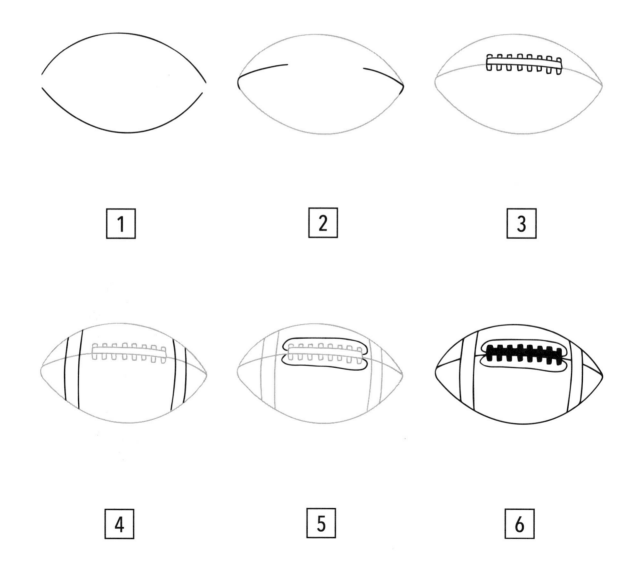

TENNIS RACKET

Before the 1960s, tennis rackets were typically made of wood. Today, tennis rackets are often made from materials like aluminum, carbon fiber, or graphite.

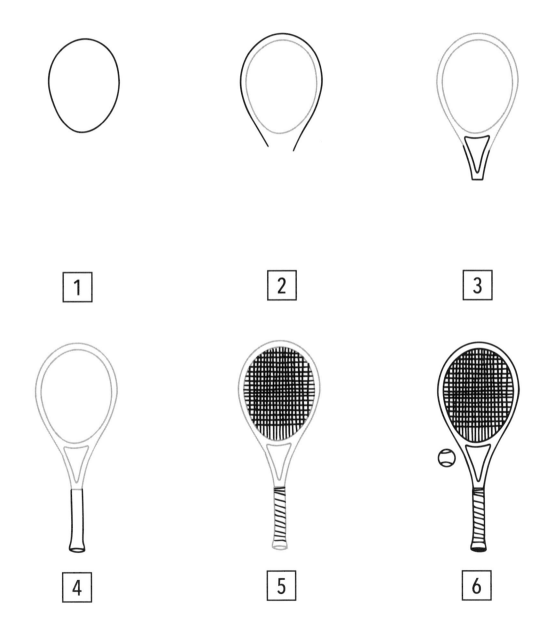

FIELD HOCKEY STICK

In field hockey, the action of moving the ball down the field with the stick is called *dribbling*.

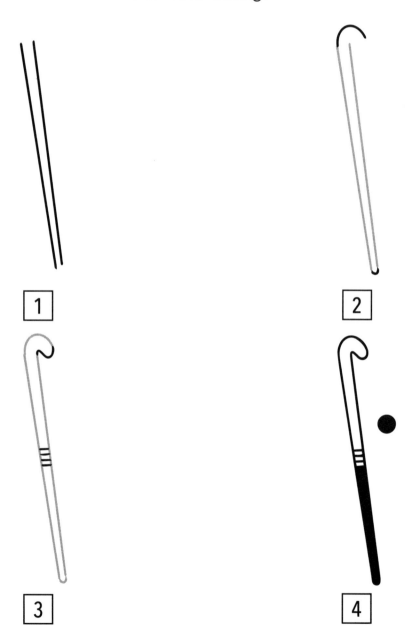

SOCCER BALL

Soccer balls are made from thirty-two different pieces sewn together: twenty of the pieces have six sides, known as *hexagons*, and twelve pieces have five sides, known as *pentagons*.

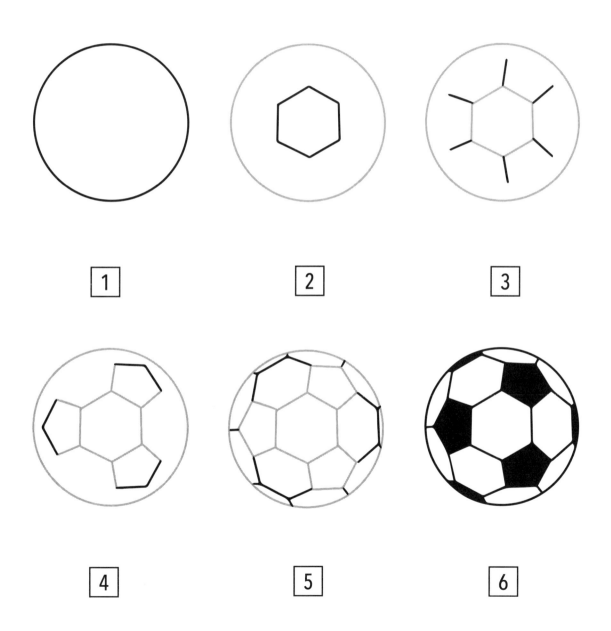

GOLF BAG

Some golfers are accompanied by a *caddie*, the name for a person in charge of carrying the player's golf bag.

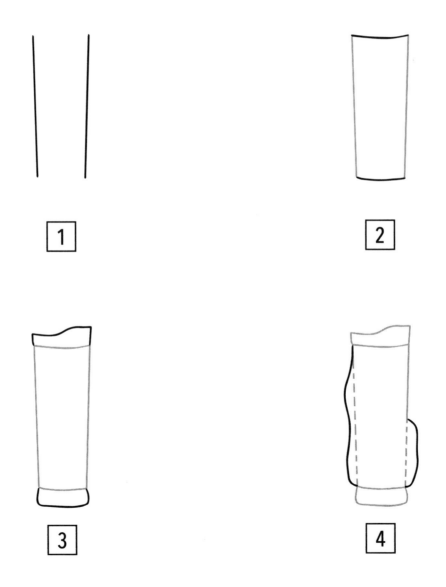

5

6

7

8

PICKUP TRUCK

In the fall, some farmers use pickup trucks to haul seasonal produce, like pumpkins, apples, and hay bales!

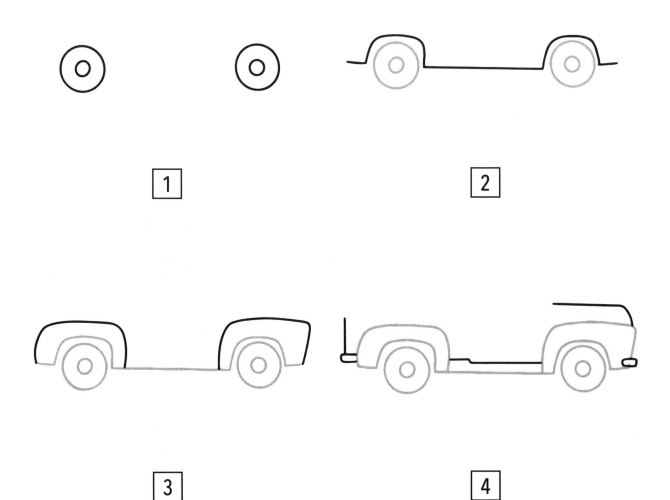

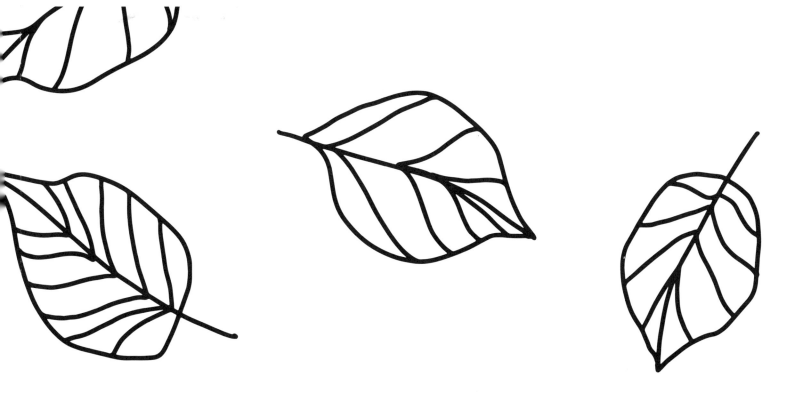

NATURE IN FALL

ACORN
Only one in 10,000 acorns will grow into an oak tree.

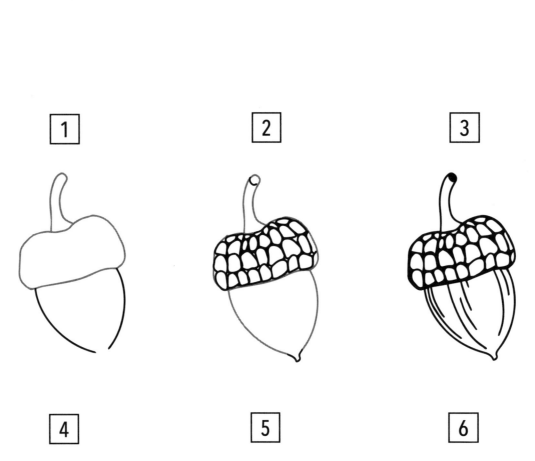

CORN

On average, an ear of corn contains 800 kernels.

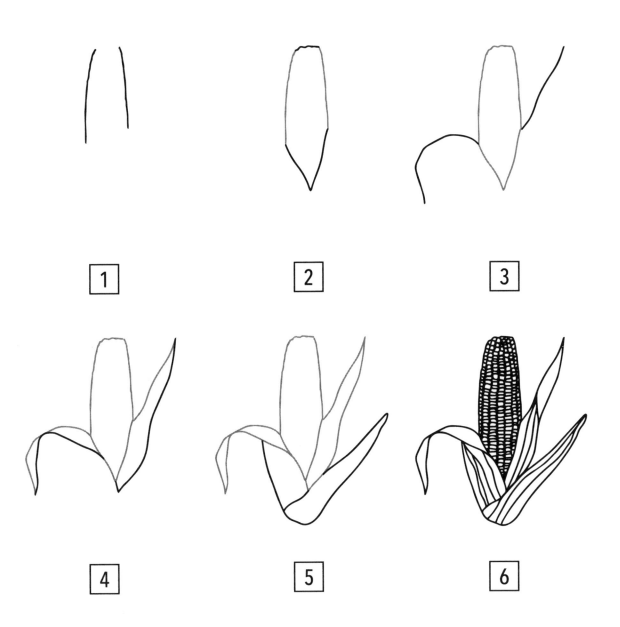

BLUEBERRIES

Blueberries are one of the only foods that are naturally blue.

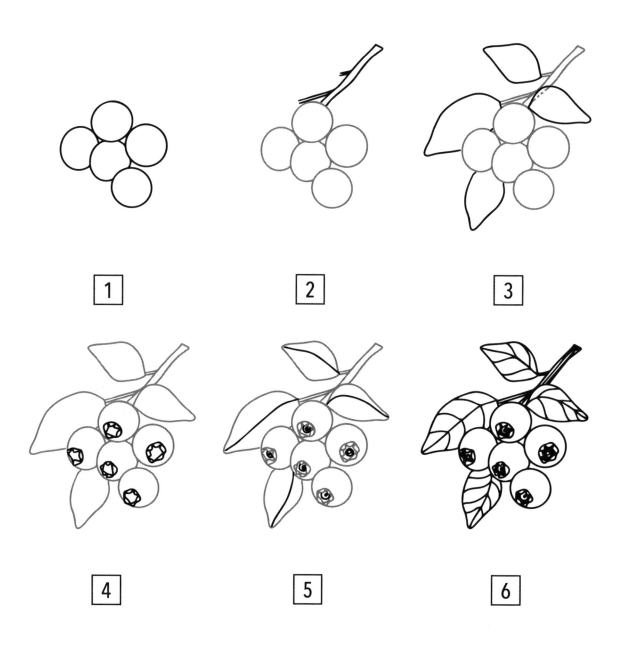

BLACKBERRIES

Blackberries are technically not berries—rather, they're made up of dozens of small fruits called *drupelets*. Each small circle you see on a blackberry is a drupelet!

PINE CONE

Coulter pine trees produce the heaviest pine cones in the world, which can weigh more than 10 pounds.

5

6

7

8

MUSHROOMS

Did you know that mushrooms aren't classified as plants? In fact, mushrooms are more closely related to humans than plants!

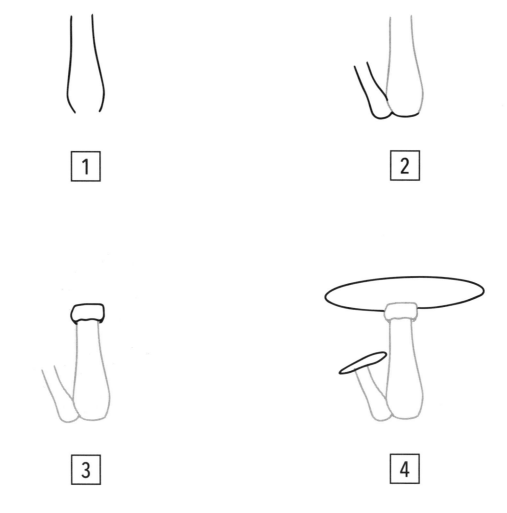

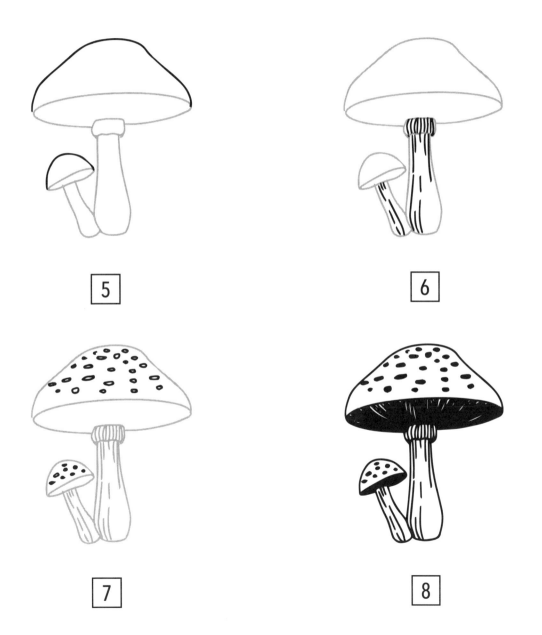

5

6

7

8

SQUIRREL
When running from predators, squirrels run in a zigzag pattern to confuse their enemies.

1

2

3

4

5

6

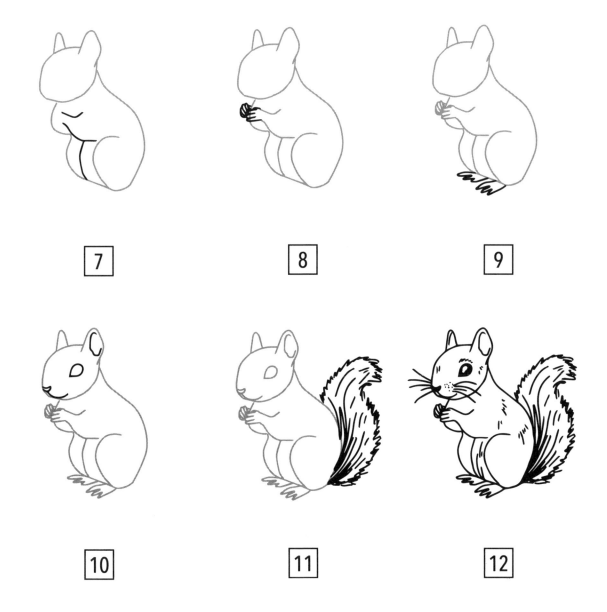

LEAF

When trees lose their leaves in the fall, it's called *abscission*. Abscission occurs when cells multiply at the base of a leaf and block the flow of nutrients, causing the leaf to fall from the tree.

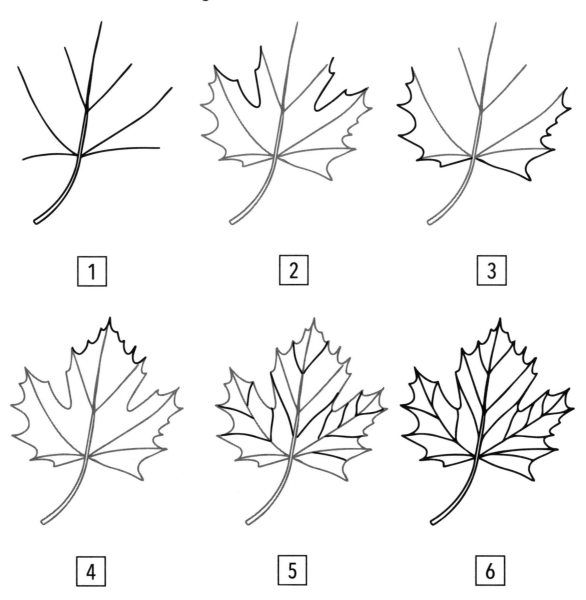

CAMPFIRE

Campfires can reach a temperature of approximately 900 degrees Fahrenheit.

41

APPLE TREE

Apples are members of the rose family, also known by its scientific name *Rosaceae*. Peaches, cherries, and pears are also members of the rose family.

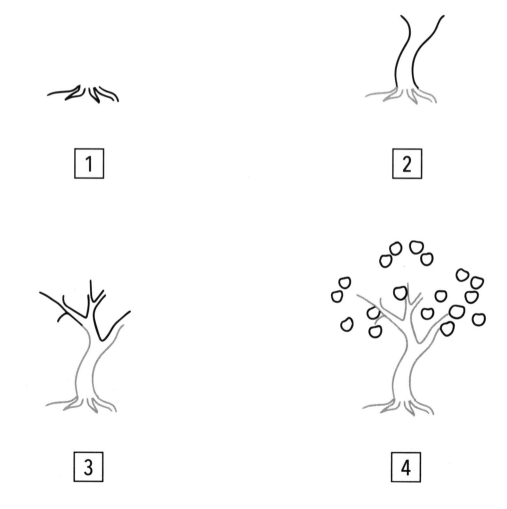

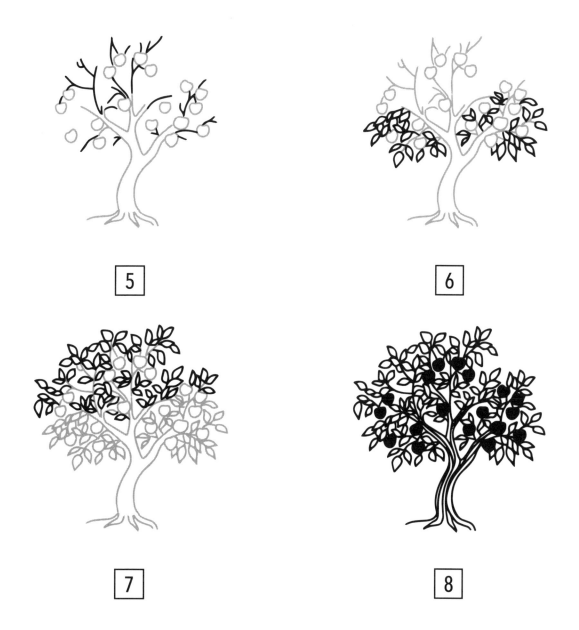

43

JACK-O'-LANTERN

According to Guinness World Records, the heaviest jack-o'-lantern weighed 2,749 pounds.

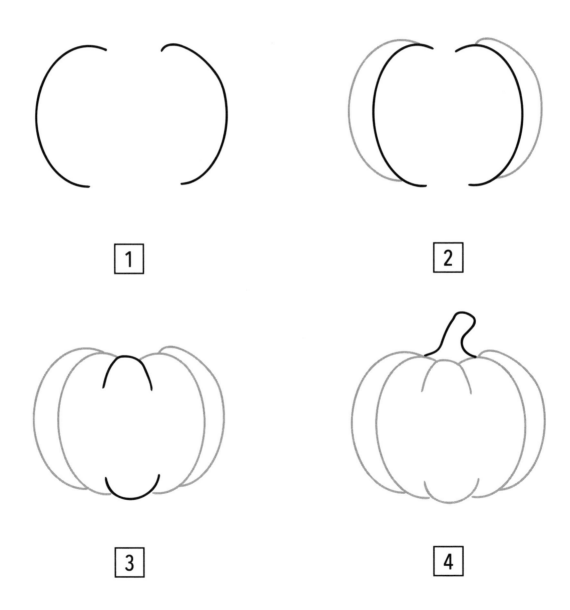

SKELETON

Humans have 206 bones in their body—106 of which are located in the hands and feet.

1

2

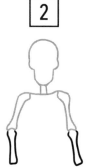

3

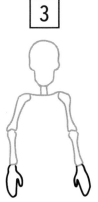

4

5

6

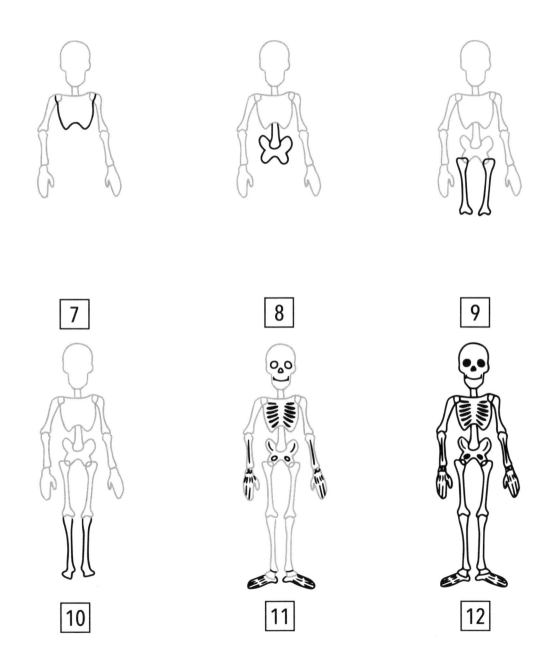

WITCH

In folklore, witches often have an animal, like a toad or a cat—known as a *familiar*—that helps protect the witch and serves as her companion.

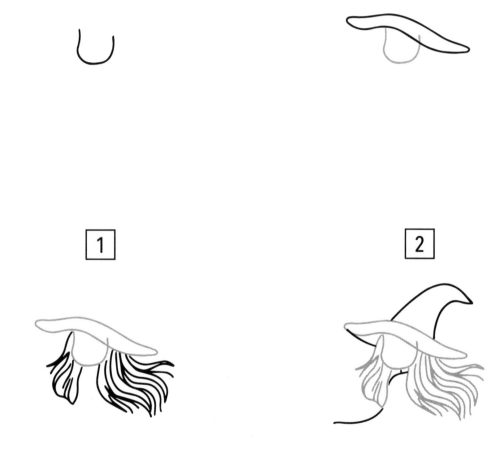

HALLOWEEN CAT
In the US, October 27 is National Black Cat Day.

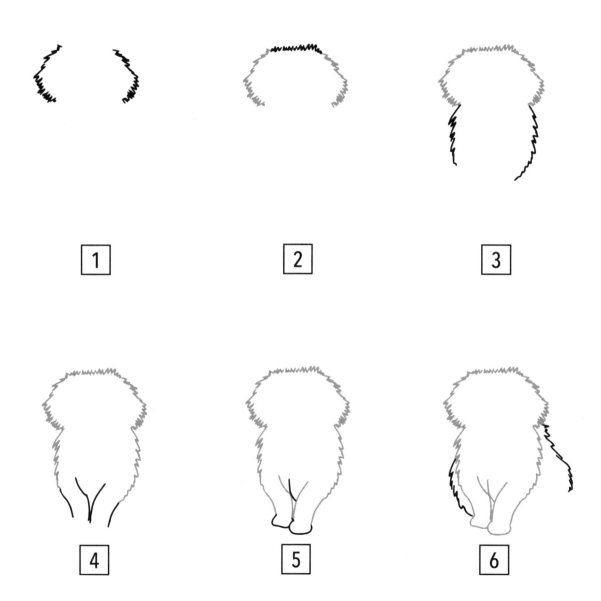

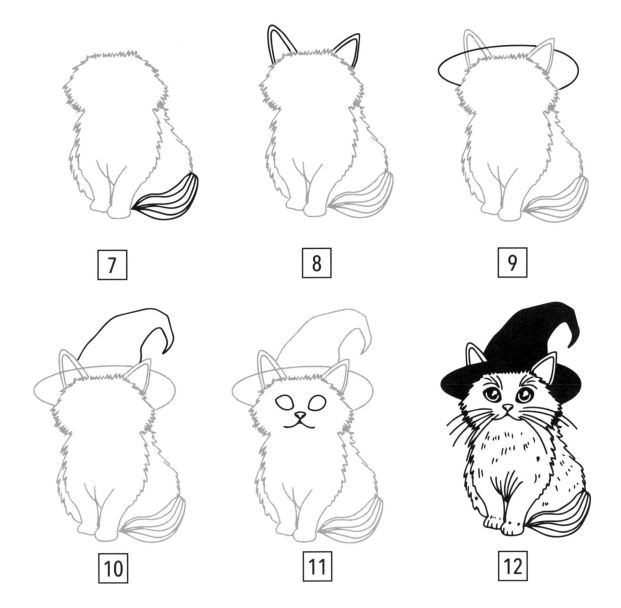

BAT

The world's smallest mammal is the Kitti's hog-nosed bat, which weighs less than a penny.

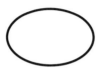

1

2

3

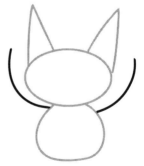

4

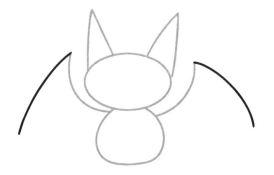

5

6

7

8

SPIDERWEB

Did you know that a strand of spider silk—which spiders use to make spiderwebs—is stronger than a strand of steel?

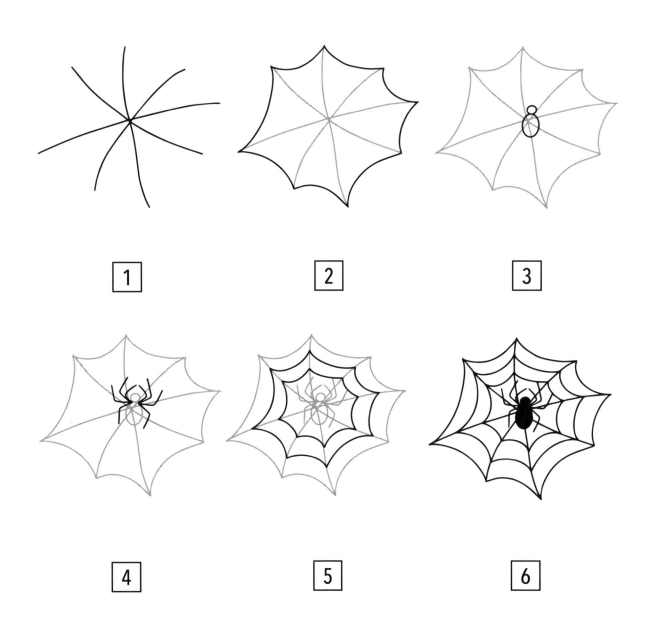

GHOST

The first known ghost story was written in 1500 BCE.
The story was inscribed on a small clay tablet.

CAULDRON

In folklore, witches often use cauldrons to concoct their potions.

MUMMY

In ancient Egypt, the most important members of society, like pharaohs, were mummified using 4,000 square feet of cloth—enough to cover a modern-day basketball court!

FRANKENSTEIN

The book *Frankenstein*, written by Mary Shelley, is considered by many to be the world's first science fiction novel.

1

2

3

4

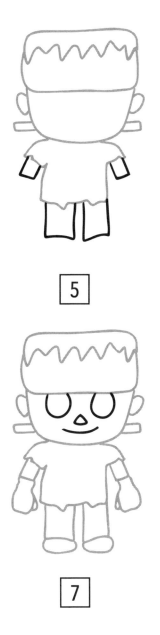

5

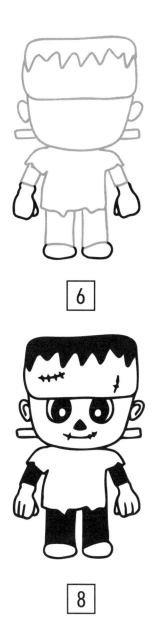

6

7

8

VAMPIRE

A group of vampires can be called a *clan*, *coven*, or *brood*.

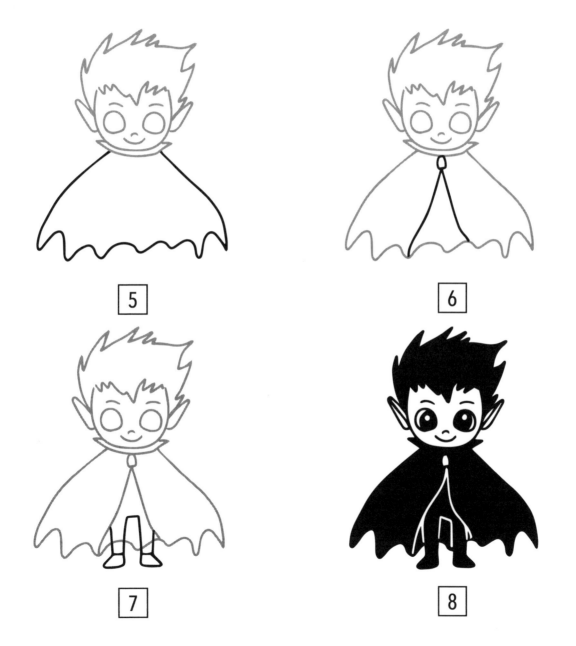

TURKEY

The skin on a turkey's neck can change color depending on their mood! When it's red, a turkey may be feeling excited or stressed. If it's blue, the turkey may be feeling calm.

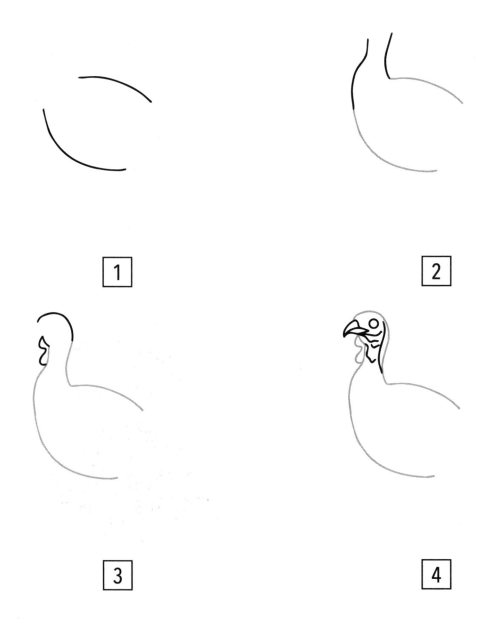

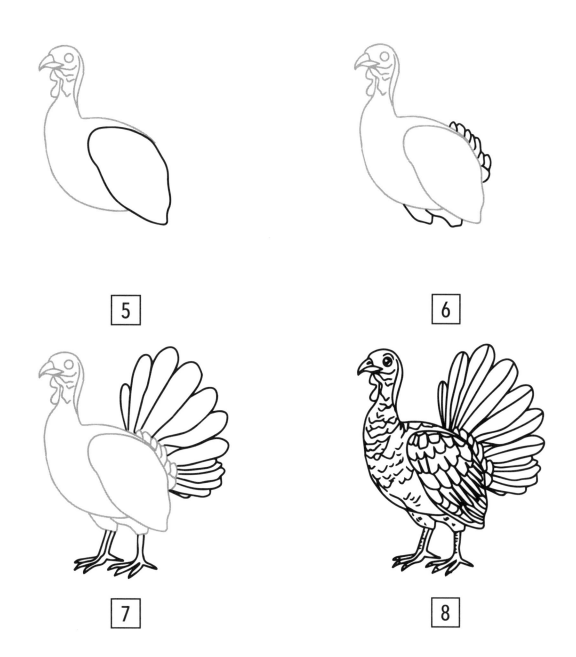

5

6

7

8

HORN OF PLENTY

The horn of plenty, also called a *cornucopia*, originates from Greek mythology and is a symbol of abundance and prosperity.

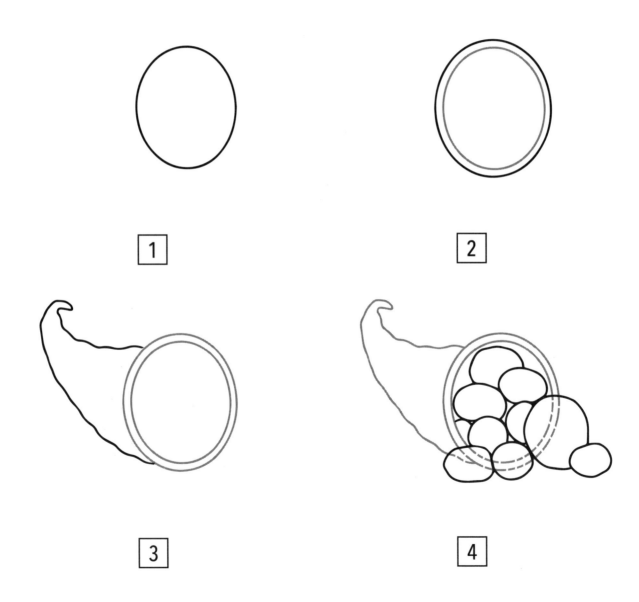

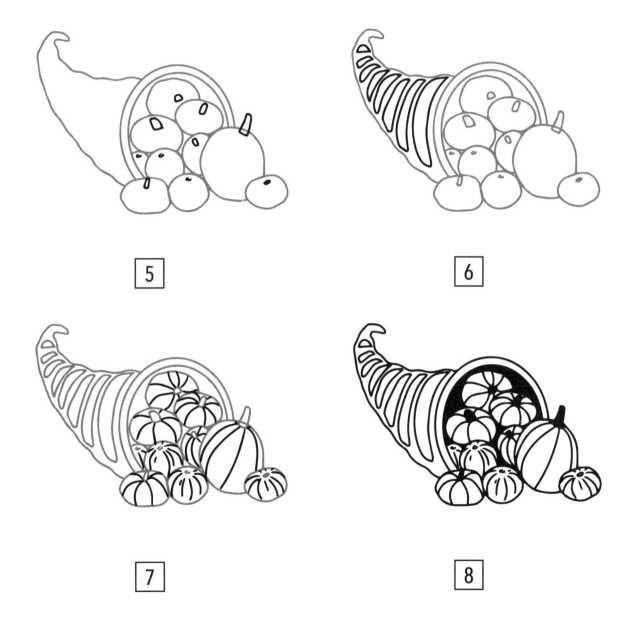

TURKEY DINNER

At the first Thanksgiving in 1621, turkey wasn't on the menu. In fact, it wasn't until the mid-1800s before it became a popular Thanksgiving dish.

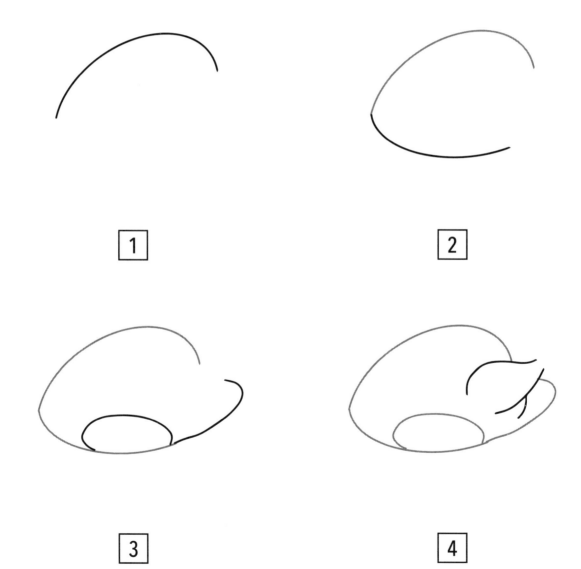

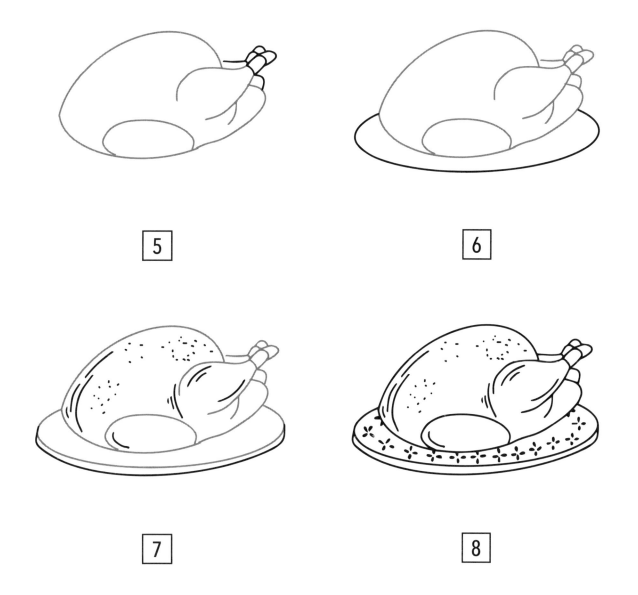

PUMPKIN PIE

The largest pumpkin pie ever made spanned 20 feet in diameter and weighed almost 3,700 pounds.

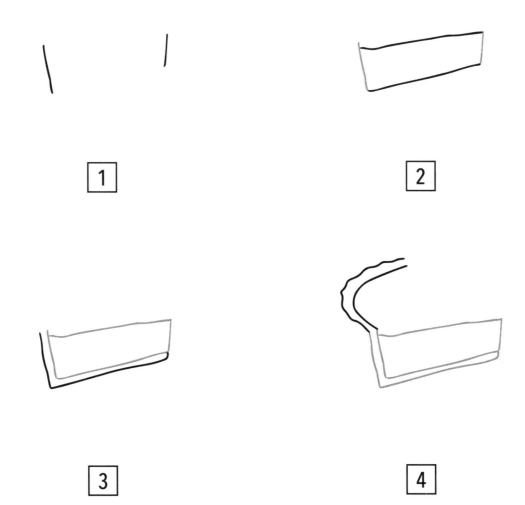

5

6

7

8

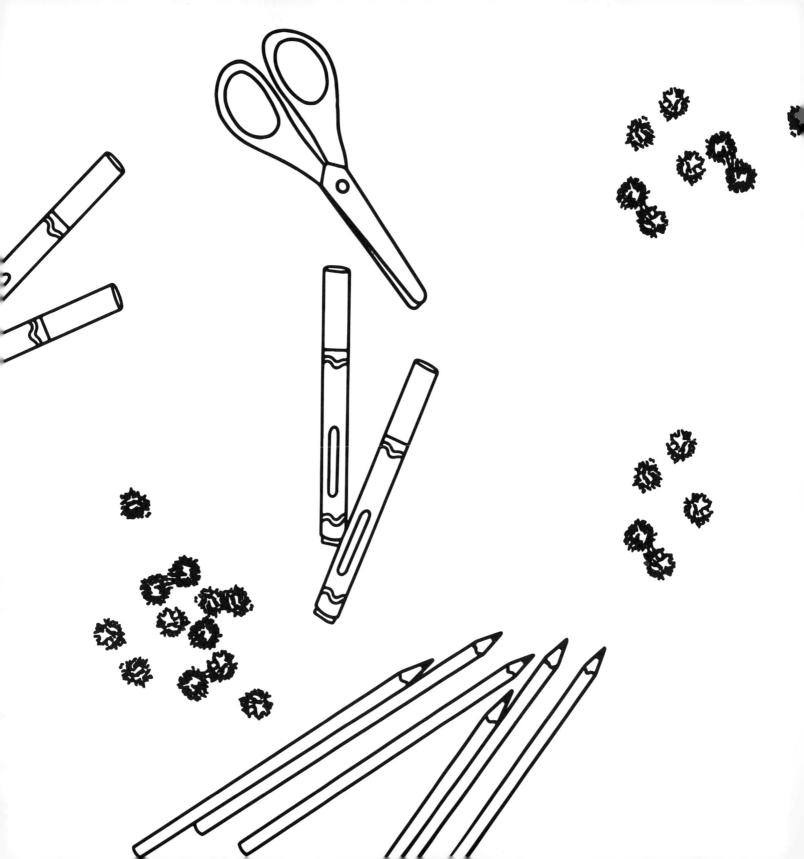

CREATE YOUR OWN

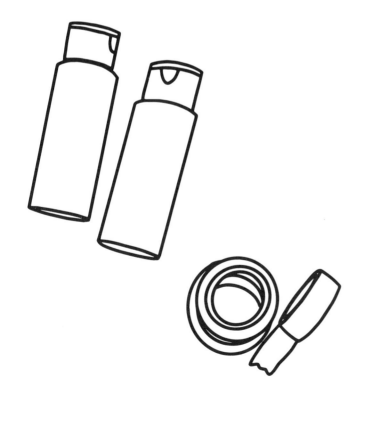

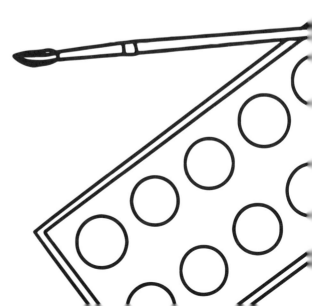

CREATE YOUR OWN PUMPKIN

Use this page to decorate a pumpkin how you would want it!

CREATE YOUR OWN FEAST

Use this page to draw a feast of your favorite foods!

CREATE YOUR OWN FALL SCENE

Fill this page with your favorite fall decorations!

About Alli K

NAME: Alli Koch

HOME: Dallas, Texas

BIRTHDAY: March 20, 1991

FAVORITE COLOR: Black

FAVORITE FOOD: Waffle fries and a large sweet tea

JOB: I am a full-time artist! I sell my art online, paint murals on the sides of buildings, and teach others how to draw or be creative.

FALL FAVORITE: Halloween festivals

PETS: I have one cat named Emmie

CAR: Two-door Jeep

FAMILY: Married to my high school sweetheart

FAVORITE THING TO DO: Play board games!